a year with marmalade

ALISON REYNOLDS • HEATH McKENZIE

The Five Mile Press

Ella and Maddy were **best friends.**

But

one

a
u
t
u
m
n
day...

everything changed.

'We're going away for a year,' said Maddy.
'Could you please look after Marmalade?'

Ella cried
and Marmalade yowled
as Maddy's family car grew

smaller

and

smaller

in the distance.

Ella
SCRUNCHED
and
toSsed
the fallen leaves,

but nobody
tossed them
back.

She picked **apples,**
but there were **too many**
for one person to crunch.
When she offered Marmalade

an apple, he batted it away.

She

S T

OMPED

through puddles,

but she was the only
one who got wet.

One
frosty
winter's morning,
Ella woke up with **warm feet**.

The pond
FROZE
OVER,

and Ella *sped around* on her skates.

SHIVERING
high up in the tree,
Marmalade gazed at her
with diamond eyes.

The days became
even colder
and Ella stayed inside.

Marmalade **swished** around Ella's legs
as she read beside the fire.

In spring Ella dug up a garden bed.

Marmalade scratched up the seeds and purred.

Ella

planted
a row
of
flowers.

Marmalade curled up on the sun-warmed earth.

One morning Ella
found a **huge** sunflower.

'Come and look Marmalade,'

she shouted.

The cat darted out.

That summer,
Ella and Marmalade
   pedalled to the beach.

They built sandcastles **bigger** than Marmalade.
Ella swam while Marmalade minded the clothes.

Autumn
returned

and so did Maddy.

Ella, Maddy and Marmalade
SCRUNCHED
through fallen leaves.

And SPLASHED through

puddles all the way home...

Ella's dad built

a special cat flap

between

Ella and Maddy's

homes.

It was just big enough

for Marmalade.

And Ella and Maddy.